Acknowledgments
The editor and publishers
would like to thank Mary Haselden for her help in
selecting rhymes for this book.

Ladybird books are widely available, but in case of
difficulty may be ordered by post or telephone from:

Ladybird Books – Cash Sales Department
Littlegate Road Paignton Devon TQ3 3BE
Telephone 0803 554761

A catalogue record for this book is available
from the British Library

Published by Ladybird Books Ltd Loughborough Leicestershire UK
Ladybird Books Inc Auburn Maine 04210 USA

numbers

illustrated by MARGARET CHAMBERLAIN

1

One little cockerel
Bright and gay,
Stood on a gate
At break of day.
"Ho, little cockerel,
How do you do?"
"Quite well, thank you.
Cock-a-doodle-doo."

One little green frog in a pond am I;
Hoppity, hoppity, hop.
I sit on a little leaf high and dry
And watch all the fishes
As they swim by –
Splash! How I make the water fly!
Hoppity, hoppity, hop.

Two little blackbirds
    singing in the sun,
One flew away
    and then there was one;
One little blackbird,
    very black and small,
He flew away
    and then there was the wall.
One little brick wall
    lonely in the rain,
Waiting for the blackbirds
    to come and sing again.

A little brown rabbit
     popped out of the ground,

Wriggled his whiskers
     and looked around.

Another wee rabbit
     who lived in the grass

Popped his head out
     and watched him pass.

Then both the wee rabbits
    went hoppity hop,

Hoppity, hoppity, hoppity, hop,

Till they came to a wall
    and had to stop.

Then both the wee rabbits
    turned themselves round,

And scuttled off home
    to their holes in the ground.

Two fat gentlemen
Met in a lane,
Bowed most politely,
Bowed once again.
How do you do?
How do you do?
How do you do again?

Two thin ladies
Met in a lane
...*etc*.

Two tall policemen
Met in a lane   ...etc.

Two little schoolboys
Met in a lane   ...etc.

Two little babies
Met in a lane
        ...etc.

Rub-a-dub-dub,
Three men in a tub,
And how do you think
They got there?
The butcher, the baker,
The candlestick-maker;
They all jumped out
Of a rotten potato,
'Twas enough to make a man stare.

Three little ghosties,
Sat on three posties,
Eating buttered toasties,
Greasing their fisties
Up to their wristies.
Weren't they beasties
To make such feasties!

Four currant buns
in a baker's shop,

Round and fat
with sugar on the top.

Along came a boy
with a penny one day,

Bought a currant bun
and took it away.

Three currant buns
in a baker's shop ...*etc.*

Two currant buns
in a baker's shop ...*etc.*

One currant bun
in a baker's shop ...*etc.*

Five little soldiers
Standing in a row,
Three stood straight,
And two stood – so.
Along came the captain,
And what do you think?
They ALL stood straight,
As quick as a wink.

Five little pussy cats
        playing near the door;
One ran and hid inside
        and then there were four.

Four little pussy cats
        underneath a tree;
One heard a dog bark
        and then there were three.

Three little pussy cats
  thinking what to do;
One saw a little bird
  and then there were two.

Two little pussy cats
  sitting in the sun;
One ran to catch his tail
  and then there was one.

One little pussy cat
  looking for some fun;
He saw a butterfly
  and then there was none.

Sing a song of sixpence,
A pocket full of rye;
Four and twenty blackbirds,
Baked in a pie.

When the pie was opened,
The birds began to sing;
Now wasn't that a dainty dish,
To set before the king?

The king was in his counting-house,
Counting out his money;
The queen was in the parlour,
Eating bread and honey.

The maid was in the garden,
Hanging out the clothes;
When down came a blackbird
And pecked off her nose.

One potato, two potato,
Three potato, four,
Five potato, six potato,
Seven potato more.

One, two, three, four,
Mary at the cottage door;
Five, six, seven, eight,
Eating cherries off a plate.

Eight brown teddies
      sitting on a wall.

Eight brown teddies
      sitting on a wall.

And if one brown teddy
      should accidentally fall,

There'd be seven brown teddies
      sitting on a wall.

Seven brown teddies
          ...etc.

Six brown teddies
          ...etc.

Five brown teddies
                    ...*etc.*

Four brown teddies
                    ...*etc.*

Three brown teddies
                    ...*etc.*

Two brown teddies
                    ...*etc.*

One brown teddy
        sitting on a wall.

And if one brown teddy
        should accidentally fall,

There'd be no brown teddies
        sitting there at all!

Higgledy Piggledy,
My black hen,
She lays eggs for gentlemen;
Sometimes nine,
And sometimes ten,
Higgledy Piggledy,
My black hen!

10

There was one little, two little,
three little Indians,
Four little, five little,
six little Indians,
Seven little, eight little,
nine little Indians,
Ten little Indian boys.

One man went to mow,
Went to mow a meadow.
One man and his dog,
     Spot, and a bottle of pop,
Went to mow a meadow.

Two men went to mow,
Went to mow a meadow.
Two men, one man and his dog,
     Spot, and a bottle of pop,
Went to mow a meadow.

Three men went to mow,
Went to mow a meadow
                    ...etc.

Who built the Ark?
Noah! Noah!
Who built the Ark?
Brother Noah built the Ark.

Now in came the animals
two by two,
The hippopotamus
and the kangaroo ...*etc.*

Now in came the animals
four by four,
Two through the window
and two through the door
...*etc.*

Now in came the animals
six by six,
The elephants laughed
at the monkeys' tricks
...*etc.*

Now in came the animals
eight by eight,

Some were on time
and some were late

...*etc.*

Now in came the animals
ten by ten,

Five black roosters
and five black hens

...*etc.*

Now Noah said,

"Go and **shut that door!**

The rain's started falling
and we can't take more."

This old man, he played one,
He played nick-nack on my drum,
With a nick-nack paddy-whack,
Give a dog a bone,
This old man came rolling home.

This old man, he played two,
He played nick-nack on my shoe
...etc.

This old man, he played three,
He played nick-nack on my knee
...etc.

This old man, he played four,
He played nick-nack on my floor
...etc.

This old man, he played five,
He played nick-nack on my hive
...etc.

This old man, he played six,
He played nick-nack on my sticks
...*etc.*

This old man, he played seven,
He played nick-nack up to heaven
...*etc.*

This old man, he played eight,
He played nick-nack at my gate
...*etc.*

This old man, he played nine,
He played nick-nack on my spine
...*etc.*

This old man, he played ten,
He played nick-nack once again
...*etc.*

One, two,
Buckle my shoe;

Three, four,
Knock at the door;

Five, six,
Pick up sticks;

Seven, eight,
Lay them straight;

Nine, ten,
A big fat hen;

Eleven, twelve,
Dig and delve;

Thirteen, fourteen,
Maids a-courting;

Fifteen, sixteen,
Maids in the kitchen;

Seventeen, eighteen,
Maids in waiting;

Nineteen, twenty,
My plate's empty.

Oh, the grand old Duke of York,
He had ten thousand men.
He marched them up
  to the top of the hill,
And he marched them down again

And when they were up
  they were up,
And when they were down
  they were down,
And when they were only
  half-way up,
They were neither up nor down.